Charlotte in London

WESTMINSTER ABBEY

Abbey Green

NAVE

BY JOAN MACPHAIL KNIGHT
ILLUSTRATIONS BY MELISSA SWEET

chronicle books · san francisco

ME and TOBY

I knew Monsieur Monet was back from Norway when I walked Toby past his garden this morning and smelled turpentine. I opened the gate and there he was with twenty canvases lined up in a row, all of the same snowy mountain in different light.

When I told him we're going to London, he put his paintbrush down and said, "J'adore Londres"—I love London. "Parfois, après la brume"—sometimes, after a fog—"the river turns to gold. C'est étonnant,"—it's remarkable—he added, and went back to his painting.

I can't wait to see that!

The Fosters are coming with us. Lizzy Foster is my best friend and we do everything together. Her father came to Giverny from Boston for the same reason mine did: to learn to paint "en plein air"—outdoors—the way the French Impressionists do. Everyone wants to study where the great master, Monsieur Monet, lives.

In London, Mama wants to have her portrait painted by the famous artist Mr. John Singer Sargent. Papa says there are so many people ahead of her, she'll be lucky to get her foot in the door. Mama says she'll find out if she can get her foot in the door when she gets there. Now she's in Paris with Mrs. Foster, shopping for shoes to wear for her London sitting.

This afternoon our cook, Raymonde, sent me to the store for bleach, "eau de javel," to whiten the tablecloths. Along the way, Toby ran into the "pâtisserie," just like always. Only this time he didn't come out with a "croissant"—he came out with my friend Hippolyte! Hippolyte told me he had come here from Paris with a friend and that I could never guess how—not if I had a hundred guesses! Then he said:

> "We came without a stop . . .
> Without a sound . . .
> Without a footstep on the ground."

"Lots of people come here by boat from Paris," I laughed.

"Pas moi!"—Not me! "Meet me at eight in the morning in Duboc's field," he said, "the one where the Americans go to try to copy Monsieur Monet's haystack paintings. Ne retarde pas!"—Don't be late!

What could it be? I wonder. I'm going straight to Lizzy's to tell her!

April 2, 1895
Rue de l'Amiscourt
Giverny

Raymonde made us a picnic lunch. I ran with the basket to Lizzy's house. When I got there, Lizzy was practicing the violin. While I waited for her to finish, I peeked into the picnic basket to see what Raymonde had made for us:

Our favorites!

poulet rôti   une baguette   du fromage   une tarte au citron

The second Lizzy finished practicing, she put her violin away and we raced to the hayfield at the edge of town. In the distance was a giant red and white balloon, decorated with flags of every color. As we got closer, we saw a basket underneath. Out stepped Hippolyte with his friend Monsieur Alberto Santos-Dumont. He's from Brazil and speaks English, French and Portuguese. He told us the balloon is named Voyageur—"Wanderer." Then he asked if we wanted to ride in it.

And we did! Up over trees and rooftops. I'll never forget what it was like to fly. It didn't feel as if we were moving at all—instead, the village seemed to slip away from us. A soft wind carried us over Lizzy's house and over our garden, where Raymonde was hanging laundry to dry. When she saw the balloon, her mouth made an O. She didn't see us—I put my hand over Toby's muzzle so he wouldn't bark and Lizzy and I hid at the bottom of the basket.

We floated above the church tower and out across fields of painters with easels and parasols (I think I saw Papa!) to the river Epte. I even saw the river Seine as far as the sea. Lizzy swore she could see the coast of England.

Monsieur Santos-Dumont said you never know where your balloon will land, and weren't we lucky to come down at the "château" of his good friend the Comte de Champfleury?

Then he let the air out of the balloon and the servants folded it up and put it inside the basket. A carriage with eight

dancing black horses pulled up to take Monsieur Santos-Dumont, Hippolyte and the balloon to Vernon to catch the train to Paris. On the way they dropped us in Giverny. We waved at them until the carriage was out of sight.

At dinner, Papa told me about the balloon he had seen and how balloons are the latest thing in London. "I hear the sky is filled with them," he said, "and that you can take a pleasure flight from any public garden." I hope that's true! In three days we'll be there!

April 8, 1895
The Savoy Hotel
Savoy Court, London

Lizzy and I love this hotel—we get to have breakfast in our room! This morning a waiter set a table with a pink cloth and napkins at our window above the river Thames. Every dish was covered with a big silver lid—even Toby's little lamb chop! We had "oeufs brouillés"—scrambled eggs—with fat croissants and strawberry jam and pitchers of hot chocolate with whipped cream. No wonder the chef is called the "King of Chefs." He's French and his name is Monsieur Auguste Escoffier. As we ate, the sun burned through the fog and the dark river turned to gold, just as Monsieur Monet said it would.

After breakfast, Lizzy went shopping with Mrs. Foster, and Papa and I went to the river— "for inspiration," Papa said, picking up his paint box. I brought my little watercolor kit. On the way we saw a giant pointy stone with carvings. Papa told me it's an obelisk and that it's called Cleopatra's Needle. Then he said it was brought here from Egypt, where it had stood for thousands of years. Buried underneath is a time capsule with photographs of the twelve most beautiful women of Great Britain. One of them is Queen Victoria. She became queen when she was only eighteen. Now she's seventy-six.

Papa found his inspiration on Westminster Bridge and rushed to set up his easel. "Look at the Houses of Parliament!" he exclaimed. I turned, and instead of buildings, factories and smokestacks on the riverbank, I saw a magical kingdom bathed in gold. Papa squeezed colors onto his palette and quickly began to paint.

alizarin crimson · vermilion · violet · Lake · cobalt blue · Black · chrome yellow

I made a watercolor.

There's as much traffic on the river as there is on the streets: steamboats, coal barges, sailboats, tugs, skiffs, crowded ferries and pleasure boats with striped awnings. We heard a bell ring twelve times and I wondered where it was. "In that clock tower," said Papa, pointing to the riverbank. "The bell is called Big Ben and it weighs more than thirteen tons. It just told us it's time for lunch." Everywhere were people selling meat pies, muffins, bread and butter, tea and pickled eels. We didn't want any of that! We went to a restaurant and had crispy fish and chips.

After we ate we went into Westminster Abbey, a giant church where England's kings and queens go to be crowned. Lots of people are buried there—more than 3,000 of them—and not just kings and queens. I saw the gravestone of a farmer named Thomas Parr. He lived to be 152!

On the way back to the hotel it started to rain. London is the city of fog, mist, smoke, rain and the river. And we saw all of that today.

Series 5033 - 3   WESTMINSTER BRIDGE, LONDON.   Davidson Brothers
LONDON.

May 2, 1895
The Savoy Hotel
Savoy Court, London

Poor Mama! Every day she stops at the hotel desk, hoping for a letter from
Mr. Sargent. She wrote him from Giverny to say she'd like her portrait painted
and that she could be reached at the Savoy Hotel, but she hasn't heard back.
Tonight we're having dinner with Mr. Whistler, a friend of Papa's from art
school in Paris. He's American but he lives in London and knows Mr. Sargent.
Mama hopes he'll have news of him.

We met Mr. Whistler at a restaurant called Simpson's next door to the hotel. Even though Papa had told Lizzy and me that Mr. Whistler loves all things Japanese, we were surprised to see he was wearing a kimono. It was very warm in the restaurant— "due," Mr. Whistler said, "to the steam of thirty thousand puddings." Lizzy and I didn't know what he meant until our dinners came: a thick slice of roast beef with a giant popover in the shape of a chef's hat, called Yorkshire Pudding. When we stuck our puddings with our forks, out came a warm puff of steam!

During dinner, Mr. Whistler told Lizzy and me that London is filled with ghosts. "I've seen the ghost of Queen Anne Boleyn," he said. "She lived more than three hundred years ago and had eleven fingers and a very long neck. Her ghost wanders the streets in a crimson gown."

After dinner, Mr. Whistler said, "Follow me," and led us to the river. On the way, Lizzy and I looked for ghosts but didn't see any. Mr. Whistler and Papa talked about how London's waste used to pour into the river until one hot summer there was a smell so terrible, everybody called it "the Great Stink." When the Great Stink reached the Houses of Parliament, Queen Victoria did something about it. She hired an engineer named Joseph Bazalgette to build 13,500 miles of sewers and drains. He hid them under embankments like the one we stood on. When he finished, she called Bazalgette a genius and made him a knight.

All at once we heard the sound of rockets going off and fireworks filled the dark sky!

Back in our room we shut the window tight. Good night, London ghosts, good night!

A London Policeman

Covent Garden Market
London

When Mama sat down to write another letter
to Mr. Sargent, I told her she should go to his studio
instead and see for herself if he's there. If he's away, maybe he left a note on
the door saying when he'll be back.

"I don't know why I didn't think of that myself," she said. First we went
to Covent Garden Market, where all of London gets its fruits, vegetables and
flowers. It was so crowded, I had to carry Toby so he wouldn't get stepped on.
While we were there, it started to rain but that didn't matter—the market
has a glass roof. Mama bought a bouquet to take to Mr. Sargent and asked
the woman how to get to Tite Street. "Want directions? Ask a bobby," the
woman said, pointing to a policeman. Mama told me policemen here are called
"bobbies," after Sir Bobby Peel, the man who started the police force.

When we left Covent Garden, the sun was out. We got on the biggest omnibus we had ever seen—two stories high. No wonder there were four big horses to pull it. We sat way up top, so we could see all of London.

When we got to 31 Tite Street, we saw a tall, thin man in a long black overcoat with a fuzzy poodle. The man said his name was W. Graham Robertson and that his dog was called Mouton, French for "sheep." "Are you here to see Mr. Sargent?" he asked. "I've been waiting over an

hour for him to come finish my portrait. It's hot in this coat, but Mr. Sargent insists I wear it. 'The coat is the picture,' he likes to say, 'the coat and the dog.'"

Just then Mouton growled at Toby but W. Graham Robertson said not to worry—"Mouton is old and nearly toothless. Mr. Sargent allows him one bite a sitting. Then he says, 'He has bitten me now, so we can go ahead,' and I know it's time for me to stand stiff as a lamppost until he says I can relax."

"Do you have any idea where Mr. Sargent might be?" wondered Mama.

"He could be on a painting holiday in Spain. Or Italy perhaps. For that matter, he could be in Egypt. He likes Egypt. We may as well go home."

Mama was quiet on the way back to the hotel. I could tell this was not what she had expected from our trip to Tite Street.

Yesterday Mama and I went to call on Mrs. Cyprian Williams. She and her husband are art collectors and very rich. She's one of those mothers who think children should be seen and not heard. Her daughters played with their Japanese dolls and didn't say a word the whole time we were there. I walked around and looked at paintings. I saw lots of portraits of Mrs. Williams but not one signed by Mr. Sargent.

I heard her tell Mama that she had gotten Mr. Sargent to agree to paint her portrait, but when he insisted she wear a dress that was two sizes too big she changed her mind. Then she said she was planning a dinner party at the Savoy Hotel and would we like to come? "Of course, you and the Fosters will receive proper invitations," she told Mama. I was glad when the visit was over. But I can't wait for the dinner party!

Back at the hotel we found Papa pacing the floor. "It's too foggy to paint," he said. "How would you like to see some paintings at the National Gallery?"

We stepped outside and Papa put a whistle to his lips. Two blasts and a gray horse came trotting out of the fog pulling a small black cab with two wheels. "One blast of the whistle would get us a four-wheeler, called a 'growler,'" said Papa, "but the hansom cab is just right for two—and by far the quickest way to get around town."

When we got to Trafalgar Square, we could barely see the museum through the fog. And we couldn't see any pigeons but we heard the flutter of their wings as we stepped down from the carriage.

We stood a long time in front of a painting by J. M. W. Turner called <u>Rain, Steam, and Speed</u>. Papa says Mr. Turner was called "the painter of light" and that when he died and left this painting to the museum, the world had never seen a picture like it. I can see why—it looks so real, I thought I should jump out of the way of the speeding train.

Mr. and Mrs. Cyprian Williams
request the pleasure of your company
at a dinner dance

EIGHT O'CLOCK
THE TWELFTH of JUNE

The Savoy
Savoy Court, London

June 12, 1895
The Savoy Hotel
Savoy Court, London

Tonight was Mrs. Cyprian Williams's dinner party. Lizzy and I had so much fun—we danced ourselves dizzy!

Two long tables were set with pink tablecloths and pink and white lilies. Everything sparkled: the crystal, the silver, the champagne—and the guests!

I could tell that Mama was happy to be seated next to the famous writer Mr. Henry James. He's the person who brought Mr. Sargent to London and gave a big party to introduce him to what Mama calls "le beau monde"—high society. Mr. James told a favorite story of Mr. Sargent's: A friend of the Duke of Portland's happened to look through the window of the duke's house and tap on the glass to get the duchess's attention. Later, when he saw the duchess, he asked her why she had so rudely ignored him. "Of course," Mr. James went on, "what he had seen was not the duchess but Sargent's portrait of the duchess!"

The famous French actress Miss Sarah Bernhardt excused herself early from the table—she had a play to star in. When she walked by, we saw that she had three little live chameleons on tiny gold leashes pinned to her dress. I wonder what they like to eat!

When Mr. Whistler saw *the* chameleons, he said, "I hear she has a pet snake and a lion, too. Not only that—people say she sleeps in a coffin."

I love lobster, so I ordered "Homard Thermidor" and Lizzy had her favorite, "Suprêmes de Volaille"—chicken with cream sauce. And since we both like potatoes, we shared "Pommes Anna," a yummy French potato cake.

Then out came dessert—"crêpes Suzette"—thin pancakes with orange sauce. Monsieur Escoffier served it himself. "Bon appétit!" he said. Enjoy your dessert! And we did!

Even though we're in our beds . . .
We still hear waltzes in our heads.

THE SILENT HIGHWAY

The Tower of London

June 15, 1895
The Savoy Hotel
Savoy Court, London

Mama and Mrs. Foster took us to the Tower of London today to see the Crown Jewels. The tower is a fortress with a drawbridge and a moat to keep people out, and when it was built, 800 years ago, it was the tallest building in London. There are guards, called "Yeoman Warders," who wear suits of red, black and gold.

No wonder kings and queens keep their jewels in the tower—they must be very safe there.

When Lizzy and I had seen enough jewels, we went outside to explore. We found a Yeoman Warder feeding some ravens. They eat raw meat and eggs, including the shells. He told us he was the raven master and that every night he whistles the ravens up to bed in their nests in the tower, where they're safe from foxes. "There have always been ravens here," he said, "and there always will be. Legend has it that if the ravens leave, the tower will crumble and the kingdom with it."

We looked down at boats on the river Thames and he pointed to a big ship. "Watch what happens when that ship reaches the bridge," he said. We did and saw the bridge open to let the ship sail through. Then it closed back up again. "Tower Bridge," he said. "She's brand-new and the pride of London." I had never seen a bridge move before!

Back at the hotel there was a letter for Mama:

Tower Bridge, London.

Follow the Thames upriver to the rowing races at the Henley Royal Regatta. Look for a tall man wearing white flannels with a silk scarf (usually striped) around his waist and a straw hat with a colored ribbon (often red). Oh, and Sargent whistles and paces back and forth while he paints. You can't miss him. Good Luck!

Henry James

We'll take a train there—the Great Western. Lizzy and I can't wait!

PICCADILLY

June 27, 1895
The Savoy Hotel
Savoy Court, London

First thing this morning, Mama and I went to Fortnum and Mason, grocers to the Queen, to pick up a picnic lunch to take to the boat races. It's on a street with a funny name—Piccadilly! I've never seen a grocery store with chandeliers and fountains before. They have everything a queen could want—I counted fifty different kinds of marmalade. We left with a picnic basket filled with chicken pies, cheeses and biscuits, chocolate truffles and two fruit tarts: strawberry and apricot. No wonder that's one of Queen Victoria's favorite shops!

104. HENLEY-ON-THAMES, ENGLAND

June 28, 1895
Henley-on-Thames

We sat on the mossy riverbank to watch the races and have our picnic. The Thames is clear and narrow here. And the air smells so sweet, you would never know it's the same river that flows through London.

We saw geese and herons—no swans, though. With so many boats here for the races they had to move them to a safe place until the regatta is over. All the wild swans on the Thames belong to the Queen. She has a man called a "Swan Marker" who wears a scarlet uniform. He keeps track of how many cygnets, baby swans, are born each year so that the Queen knows exactly how many swans she has.

While we ate, Papa and Mr. Foster talked about the light and the river. And about an American painter named Mr. Frank Millet, who lives up in the Cotswolds, in the village of Broadway. "Lots of artists are there," said Papa. "They say it's England's Giverny."

Just then Toby saw a little dog in a boat and ran barking along the riverbank. Lizzy and I ran after him. We saw a man with an easel and tiptoed around behind him to see what he was painting. He wasn't wearing white flannels, but the painting was so beautiful, I asked him if he was Mr. Sargent. He smiled and put down his palette and brush. "What a compliment!" he said. "No, I'm not Mr. Sargent. My name is Lavery, John Lavery. Mr. Sargent was just here, though. He made a painting right over there—left about an hour ago." We won't tell Mama. She would be much too disappointed.

July 2, 1895
The Savoy Hotel
Savoy Court, London

When we opened the curtains this morning, the sun was shining. The Fosters are spending the day at the river Thames but Papa says he has made enough river paintings. So he rented a carriage for the day—emerald green with gold trim and four black horses to pull it. "Hyde Park!" he called out to the driver and off we went.

On the way we passed one of the biggest buildings I've ever seen. The driver slowed the horses to a walk and pointed to it with his whip. "That's Buckingham Palace," he said, "home to Queen Victoria and her nine children. But don't go looking for them. The Queen decided she likes the country better, so it's at Windsor Castle that you'll find her. Or at Balmoral, up in Scotland, now that summer's here." Then he cracked his whip and took us to Hyde Park.

62. — LONDON — BUCKINGHAM PALACE

102. ROTTEN ROW. LONDON, ENGLAND

Papa said that when Henry VIII was king, he made Hyde Park his hunting ground. It was filled with deer, birds and wild boar. Now Hyde Park is filled with ladies on bicycles. "Wearing the latest fashion, I see," said Mama. "Divided skirts, made especially for cycling."

Papa had the carriage stop at Speaker's Corner, where men on stepladders were shouting. "Anyone can stand up and say anything he likes here," said Papa. "Except about the Queen, of course—this is, after all, a royal park."

Suddenly the sky turned dark and it started to pour. "Marylebone Road!" cried Papa. "No one should leave London without visiting Madame Tussaud's."

"Leave London?" I asked. Papa explained that he had lots of London canvases and was ready to move on—to the village of Broadway he keeps hearing about. The Fosters will join us there later.

Madame Tussaud was a French lady who made figures of famous people out of candle wax and used human hair on their heads. I thought the figures were real when we first walked into the room, and I kept waiting for them to breathe or speak. It's very dark in there because sunlight would melt them. I saw a figure wearing a crimson gown and thought it might be Queen Anne Boleyn—when I counted her fingers, I knew it was!

We leave for Broadway the day after tomorrow. Papa says it will take us sixteen hours to get there and that we'll make the trip in two days. I hope I'll like it there. I'll miss Lizzy and the Savoy Hotel and Monsieur Escoffier's cooking.

July 5, 1895
The Sow and Acorn
Somewhere in the Cotswolds

We're on our way to Broadway by coach. One of the other passengers is an American painter. His name is Mr. Edwin Abbey and he's going as far as Fairford. That's where we'll change horses and spend the night.

Right now we're waiting for our lunch at a pub called "The Sow and Acorn." Papa and Mr. Abbey are having steak and ale pie, Mama isn't hungry and I'm having my favorite, fish and chips!

Lynton, Cherry Bridge.

MENU

 = COTSWOLDS

After lunch a man and a little girl got into the coach. Every time she saw a herd of sheep, the girl shouted, "Sheeps! Sheeps!"—all the way to Fairford. Mr. Abbey says that sheep pens are called "cots" here and rolling hills are "wolds." Now I know why this part of England is called "the Cotswolds."

Mr. Abbey met us at the hotel for dinner. He told us about the time he and his friend Mr. Sargent were on a boat on the Thames and Mr. Sargent dove into the water and hit his head on something. After Mr. Sargent's head was bandaged, Mr. Abbey took him up to Broadway to recover, and Mr. Sargent has been painting in the Cotswolds ever since.

Then he handed Papa a small package wrapped in brown paper to take to Mr. Millet.

July 7, 1895
The Lygon Arms
Broadway

It's very cozy in our room. Before we went to bed, Papa lit a fire. Then I heard an owl hoot and the next thing I knew there was a knock on the door and breakfast was here.

After breakfast, Papa said he was going to Russell House to see Mr. Millet, and did I want to come? When we got there, we saw a boy with a fat woolly ram on a rope. Toby barked and the ram lowered his horns and pawed the ground with his hoof. I held on to Toby as tightly as I could. The boy said his name was Laurence Millet and that the ram was called Homer. "My father's in his studio," he said. "I'll take you there." He led us through a garden filled with pink roses, scarlet poppies and hollyhocks the colors of sunset.

I saw a tower covered with ivy, a lily pond and a court for lawn tennis.

When we came to a big barn, we found
Mr. Millet cleaning his brushes. Papa handed him
the package from Mr. Abbey. He opened it to find
several tubes of paint.

"Cadmium yellow! I'm always running out of
this," he said. "At certain times of day the entire
village looks as if it's been dipped in golden honey—
including the sheep."

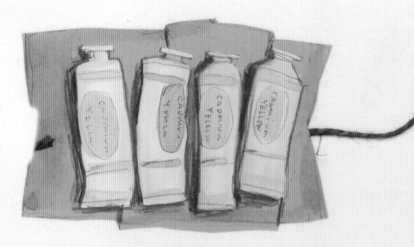

While they talked, I looked around the
biggest studio I had ever seen. I saw racks of
beautiful costumes, wigs, musical instruments—even
pianos and harpsichords. And everywhere easels
with paintings on them, some finished, some not.
I stopped at one of them—a large canvas of a boy in
a sailor suit. The boy looked familiar. Could it be?
I wondered.

"Is that Hippolyte?" I asked. "Why, yes," said Mr. Millet, "do you know him? He came with his uncle, Monsieur Durand-Ruel, an art dealer, who was here to look at paintings for his London gallery. They'll be back next Saturday for dinner. Would you like to join us?" Papa says that one can and should expect anything of life, but I never, ever expected this!

STREET. BROADWAY

July 18, 1895
The Lygon Arms
Broadway

Mama hears that some guests of the Millets' wear costumes to dinner. "I'll wear a hat with camellias," she said, "like the one I saw in London."

She took a plain straw hat to the village hatmaker and had her sew red camellias and a pink ribbon around the crown. Today we went to pick it up. Mama looks beautiful in it. We bought velvet ribbons for my hair—midnight blue.

After, we went to a tearoom and had English cream tea: scones with clotted cream—a cream so thick I could stand my spoon in it.

le paon

July 20, 1895
The Lygon Arms
Broadway

Tonight was the Millets' party. The garden was lit with Japanese lanterns. Everybody was drinking champagne and eating pigs in blankets—little sausages wrapped in pastry. Suddenly there was a loud screeching sound and all the little children ran for the house.

"C'est le paon," said a voice behind me—it's the peacock. "Il n'aime pas les petits"—he doesn't like little children. I turned and saw Hippolyte standing there with a girl with a crown of flowers on her head. She said her name was Tessa Gosse. Then she disappeared and came back with a crown of flowers for me and a crown of laurel leaves for Hippolyte. Once the children were inside the house, the peacock stopped screeching and we went in to dinner.

The little children were already seated at their table. When I found my place card, I was glad to see I was sitting next to Hippolyte. Mr. Henry James was at our table, too. I could tell he was having a good time—he said "How jolly!" over and over again.

We had salmon from Scotland, peas from the garden and Beef Wellington—roast beef in a pastry crust. While we waited for dessert, Hippolyte taught me the French words for the flowers in my crown. Then out came the strawberries and cream.

la couronne
de Charlotte

les bluets
les marguerites
les œillets
les myosotis

I heard Mr. Sargent's name mentioned and listened carefully. Mr. Augustus Saint-Gaudens, the sculptor, was talking about how Mr. Sargent had painted a portrait of his son. "Whenever the boy grew restless and squirmed, Sargent simply sat on him to keep him still," he laughed.

Then Hippolyte whispered, "Je sais où il y a des Gitans"—I know where there are Gypsies. "I'll take you there tomorrow." And I could think of nothing else.

July 21, 1895
The Lygon Arms
Broadway

This morning on our way to the Gypsy camp, Hippolyte pointed out things I'd never seen before: wild orchids in the woods, flowers called "scarlet pimpernels" and yellow "cowslips"—yellow frogs, too! We crossed a meadow filled with rabbits—they hopped off in all directions when they heard us coming. And we saw a girl picking cabbages "pour faire de la soupe," said Hippolyte—to make a soup. "By the way," he added, "the Gypsy word for rabbit is 'shooshi.'"

We came to the edge of a wood and smelled food cooking. "I bet that's 'ragôut de hérisson'"—hedgehog stew—said Hippolyte, sniffing the air. Then he told me the Gypsy word for hedgehog—"hotche withchi"—and the recipe for hedgehog stew: "First they wrap the hedgehog in wet clay. Then they cook it over a fire. When it's done, they crack the clay open and pull it away and the spines come with it."

I was about to ask how he knew so much about Gypsies when we got to their camp. There were dogs and children around the campfire and, tethered nearby, spotted horses with furry, feathery feet. Gypsies have the most beautiful wagons I've ever seen, painted bright colors and covered with designs—even the little stairs leading up to the wagons are decorated with shapes, stars and swirls. Hippolyte says a Gypsy owns his wagon forever and that no one else can ever live in it. When a Gypsy dies, his wagon is burned.

Just then the dogs began to bark. A man pulled aside the curtain at the back of his wagon and stuck his head out. We didn't stop running until we got to the rabbit meadow!

I have so much to tell Lizzy when I see her next week.

July 28, 1895
The Lygon Arms
Broadway

When Papa went to the Millets' today to paint, I went with him. There was a game of lawn tennis—artists against writers. We stayed to cheer the artists, but Mr. Edmund Gosse, a poet, and Mr. Henry Harper, who owns <u>Harper's Magazine</u>, won. Then we set our easels up in the garden and got to work. I squeezed the colors of a Cotswold summer onto my palette:

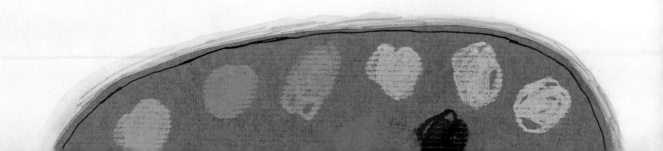

All at once I heard Toby barking behind the greenhouse. There was a tiny yellow bird lying on the ground. It must have flown into the glass. I held the bird in my hands a moment—then it fluttered its wings and flew away.

I turned to go back to my painting and heard a man say, "Wait! Stay just as you are." He was very tall and stood behind an easel with a small canvas on it. He looked a long time at Toby and me and started to paint. Then he walked forward and back, whistling as he went. "At last I found you, Mr. Sargent!" I thought.

I'm used to posing for Papa so I know to stand very still. Mr. Sargent paints quickly and keeps his paints in a fruit basket rather than a paint box. When he finished, he held the canvas up for me to see. The painting looked so real, it was like looking into a mirror.

When I told Mr. Sargent that we had traveled all the way to London from Giverny so he could paint Mama's portrait, he said he promised himself he would never paint another formal portrait. "I'm sick and tired of people who insist that I paint their portrait and have sitting after sitting and complain when they see what they look like once the painting is finished," he said. "So now the garden is my studio and I paint what I please."

He looked around. "The light's fading," he said. "Time for my evening ride. Wish me luck—I'm no better on horseback than I am on a bicycle. I always fall off at least once! By the way, thanks for posing," he called over his shoulder.

When I told Papa, he said I had been in the presence of a great man. "Sargent may be famous for his portraits," he added, "but it's in his landscapes that you see his genius. He was painting en plein air in Giverny with Monet long before we thought about going there. They're still the best of friends."

Papa turned and looked out the window. "Sargent's paintings of the canals in Venice and the gardens of Tuscany are without equal," he said. Then he looked at me and smiled. "We should go to Italy some time."

Papa has found us a beautiful cottage with big stone fireplaces and window seats for reading. There's a well in the front garden with water that heals sick eyes and ears. At least that's what people in the village say. And a thatched roof, made of straw. Papa says every thatcher has his own pattern and that you can tell who thatched a roof just by looking at it. Best of all, our cottage will have the Fosters in it this afternoon—they're on their way and I can't wait!

It's been a while since I've written—Lizzy and I are so busy. Today we took a picnic to the Vale of Evesham. On the way we passed a church filled with white lilies. We could tell the church was built with money from selling sheep's wool. In the stained-glass window it says:

"I thank my God and ever shall
It is the sheep hath paid for all."

A lady told us they were getting ready for a wedding. "Listen for wedding bells around three o'clock," she called to us when we left. Later, as we ate cucumber sandwiches, we heard bells ringing through the woods.

When we got back to Badger Bosk, there was laughter outside the back door. We opened it and saw three Gypsy girls selling clothes pegs. One of them was the girl from the cabbage patch. She smiled when she saw me. I asked her name. "Esmeralda," she said.

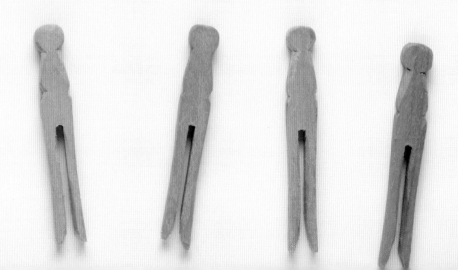

September 4, 1895
Badger Bosk
Broadway

Tonight we were invited to Russell House for cake, biscuits and champagne to celebrate the birthday of Tessa's father, Mr. Gosse. But first we had dinner with the Fosters at the Lygon Arms—roast goose with applesauce. And for dessert, raspberry fool. The chef told us how he makes it. I wrote the recipe down for Raymonde.

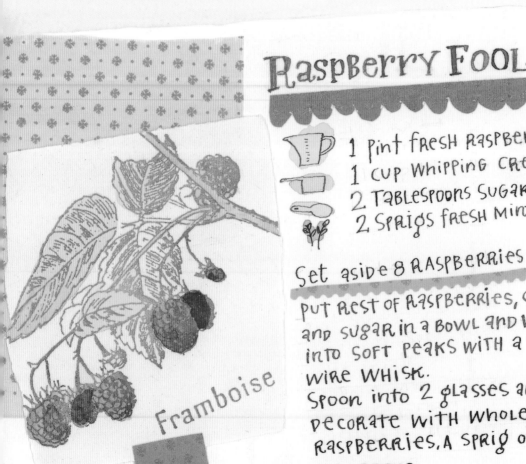

Raspberry Fool for two

- 1 pint fresh raspberries
- 1 cup whipping cream
- 2 tablespoons sugar
- 2 sprigs fresh mint

Set aside 8 raspberries

Put rest of raspberries, cream and sugar in a bowl and whip into soft peaks with a wire whisk.
Spoon into 2 glasses and chill. Decorate with whole raspberries, a sprig of mint, and serve.

Framboise

Then the chef told us about the ghost. "He sits here and has himself a pint of bitters," he said. "And when he's finished, he up and walks through that wall where the fireplace is. There's no door there now," he added, "but two hundred years ago there was. Ghosts are creatures of habit!" he laughed. Lizzy and I saw lots of men drinking beer but not one of them left through the wall.

When we got to Russell House, we followed the sounds of music and laughter to the barn. The gaslights were turned up and people were playing cards, having their palms read and dressing up in costumes for charades. Mr. Sargent was singing and playing the piano; another man, the trombone. Mr. Abbey put on a red wig and a skirt and danced the Virginia reel while Mr. Millet did a jig.

Mr. Saint-Gaudens cut silhouettes of Lizzy and me from black paper. Then he put them up on the wall—two more silhouettes in a long line of guests who have come to Russell House. After Mr. Gosse opened his presents, Papa said it was time to go home—he didn't want another late night and hoped to get some painting in tomorrow before the sun was too high in the sky.

September 15, 1895
Badger Bosk
Broadway

Today Mr. Alfred Parsons, a friend of Mr. Henry James's, rented a steam
launch and we all spent the day on the Avon River. Mr. James says Mr.
Parsons is a gardener extraordinaire as well as a painter. I can see why—Mr.
Parsons trims the hedgerows at his estate, Luggers Hall, into perfect fat shapes—
an art called "topiary," Papa told me.

      Papa and Mr. Foster rented dogcarts to take us to Evesham, where the
boat is. Lizzy and I rode with Papa and the art supplies. I thought a dogcart was
a small cart pulled by a large dog but it's not—it's a cart that's pulled by a pony.
It's big enough for four people with room under the seat for a hunting dog or two.
Since Toby isn't a hunting dog, he sat on my lap.

la fougère

le champignon

le ruisseau

A table ran the entire length of the boat, set with the biggest picnic lunch Lizzy and I had ever seen: goose, ham, chicken, meat pies, pickled walnuts and cakes, biscuits and pies—fruit tarts, too. Mr. Abbey played the banjo while we helped ourselves.

We motored up the river until we came to a landing, where everybody got out to paint—or to explore, like Lizzy and me. Mama sat by a brook lined with ferns while Lizzy and I walked upstream. I was surprised to hear someone call my name. It was Mr. Sargent, peering around a small easel.

"That's your mother, isn't it?" he asked. I nodded and then he turned the painting around so I could see it. It was of Mama and so beautiful I couldn't speak.

On the way back the sky turned gray and the air chilly. When we got off the boat, Mr. Sargent handed me the painting. "I hope your mother likes it," he said. "She will," I thought, "more than you could ever know."

We trotted back to Broadway as quickly as our pony could take us. Lizzy and I pulled our sweaters tightly around ourselves and sat close for warmth. Papa said, "Now that the weather is changing, I'm thinking about going home."

"Home?" we said. "To Boston?"

"No, home to Giverny," answered Papa.

"Yippee!" we shouted, and we laughed and talked about what our next adventure might be.

CREDITS
In order of journal entry

April 2, 1895
Theodore Robinson (1852–1896)
The Young Violinist (Margaret Perry), c. 1889.
Oil on canvas, 32 1/16 x 26 1/16 inches. The Baltimore Museum of Art: The Cone Collection, formed by Dr. Claribel Cone and Miss Etta Cone of Baltimore, Maryland BMA 1950.290.

April 8, 1895
Claude Monet (1840–1926)
The Thames at Charing Cross, 1903.
Oil on canvas, 28 3/4 x 39 1/2 inches.
Musée des Beaux-Arts, Lyon. Photograph ©
Giraudon/The Bridgeman Art Library.

**Giuseppe (or Joseph) De Nittis
(1846–1844)**
Westminster, 1878. Oil on canvas, 45 1/4 x 77 1/2
inches. Gaetano Marzotto Collection, Italy/
The Bridgeman Art Library.

May 2, 1895
James McNeill Whistler (1834–1903)
Nocturne in Black and Gold, the Falling Rocket,
c. 1875. Oil on wood panel, 23 3/4 x 18 3/8
inches. The Detroit Institute of Arts, Gift of
Dexter M. Ferry, Jr. Photograph © 2001
The Detroit Institute of Arts/The Bridgeman
Art Library.

May 14, 1895
Sidney Starr (1857–1925)
The City Atlas, c. 1889. Oil on canvas,
24 x 20 1/16 inches. National Gallery of Canada,
Ottawa/The Bridgeman Art Library.

June 1, 1895
Philip Wilson Steer (1860–1942)
Mrs. Cyprian Williams and Her Two Little Girls,
1891. Oil on canvas, 30 x 40 1/4 inches. Tate
Gallery, London. Purchased with assistance
from anonymous subscribers, 1928. Photograph courtesy of Tate London/Art Resource,
New York.

**Joseph Mallord William Turner
(1775–1851)**
*Rain, Steam, and Speed, The Great Western
Railway,* painted before 1844. Oil on canvas,
35 3/4 x 48 inches. National Gallery, London.
Photograph © National Gallery/The Bridgeman Art Library.

June 28, 1895
Sir John Lavery (1856–1941)
Boating Scene at Maidenhead, 1913. Oil on
canvas, 40 x 50 inches. © Private Collection/
© Whitford & Hughes, London/The Bridgeman Art Library.

July 7, 1895
John Singer Sargent (1856–1925)
The Late Major E. C. Harrison as a Boy, c. 1888.
Oil on canvas, 68 x 32 7/8 inches. Southampton
City Art Gallery, Hampshire, UK/The Bridgeman Art Library.

July 20, 1895
Walter Frederick Osborne (1859–1903)
The Children's Party, 1900. Oil on canvas,
24 1/4 x 30 inches. Photograph courtesy of Pyms
Gallery, London.

July 21, 1895
Sir James Guthrie (1859–1930)
A Hind's Daughter, 1883. Oil on canvas,
36 1/8 x 30 inches. National Gallery of Scotland,
Edinburgh/The Bridgeman Art Library.

July 28, 1895
John Singer Sargent painting in the countryside, 1889. Photograph copyright © The Illustrated London News Picture Library, London/
The Bridgeman Art Library.

John Singer Sargent (1856–1925)
Portrait of Miss Dorothy Vickers, c. 1884. Oil on
canvas, 18 x 15 inches. Collection of Mr. and
Mrs. Vincent Carrozzo. Photograph courtesy
of Adelson Galleries, Inc.

September 15, 1895
John Singer Sargent (1856–1925)
The Black Brook, c. 1908. Oil on canvas,
21 3/4 x 27 1/2 inches. Tate, London. Photograph
courtesy of Tate Gallery, London/Art Resource,
New York.

All other photographs and ephemera
collection of the author.

THE ARTISTS

EDWIN AUSTIN ABBEY (1852–1911) Born in Philadelphia, Pennsylvania, Abbey was a self-taught illustrator and muralist. When he was fourteen he got a job at *Harper's Weekly* in New York and later traveled to England on assignment for it. He liked London so much he decided stay on. When his friend Frank Millet moved to the village of Broadway, Abbey went with him, and they, along with John Singer Sargent, formed the nucleus of the colony of "plein air" painters that sprang up there. In 1902, Abbey was chosen as the official painter of the coronation of King Edward VII.

GIUSEPPE (OR JOSEPH) DE NITTIS (1846–1884) De Nittis came from Barletta, in the south of Italy, and studied at the art academy in Naples. He moved to Paris and, in 1874, at the invitation of Edgar Degas, participated in the first Impressionist exhibition there. A trip to London the following year inspired more Impressionist paintings, including his large canvas in this book, *Westminster*, one of ten views of the city commissioned by an English banker and patron of De Nittis.

SIR JAMES GUTHRIE (1859–1930) Guthrie was born in Greenock, Scotland, and trained as a lawyer before turning to painting. He traveled to France in 1882, where he learned to paint "en plein air." Back in Scotland, he continued to paint directly from nature and became a leading member of the Glasgow School of artists. He was made president of the Royal Scottish Academy in 1902 and was knighted the following year.

SIR JOHN LAVERY (1856–1941) Born in Belfast, Ireland, Lavery was apprenticed as a young man to a photographer in Glasgow, Scotland, where, retouching negatives and colored photographs, he decided he wanted to be a portrait painter. As a student at the Académie Julian in Paris, he was influenced by Whistler and the Impressionists, then went to London where he had an immensely successful career and painted portraits of the royal family. The face of his beautiful wife, Hazel, graced the Irish pound note until the 1970s.

FRANCIS DAVIS MILLET (1846–1912) Born in Mattapoisett, Massachusetts, Millet was a drummer boy during the Civil War. After graduating from Harvard University, he attended the Royal Academy of Fine Arts, Antwerp, Belgium. In 1895, Millet traveled to England with his wife, Lily, and their four children to live and paint in the picturesque village of Broadway, where he was soon joined by a lively group of artists and friends, including Augustus Saint-Gaudens, John Singer Sargent and the writer Henry James. In 1912, traveling to New York without his family, Millet bought a first-class ticket on the *Titanic* and went down with the ship when it struck an iceberg.

CLAUDE MONET (1840–1926) Oscar Claude Monet was born in Paris but moved to Le Havre with his family when he was five. Even as a boy, he was gifted, and he was encouraged by his parents and teachers to study art. In 1859, he returned to Paris to attend Académie Suisse. In 1862, he met Pierre-Auguste Renoir and Alfred Sisley, and together they founded an independent group of artists. They organized their first group exhibition in 1874. Monet's painting *Impression: Sunrise* gave rise to the name "Impressionism" and defined the group's style. In 1883, after his first wife, Camille, had died, Monet moved with Alice Hoschedé and her six children to Giverny. They settled into the Maison du Pressoir, or "Cider-Press House," where he lived—painting, gardening and landscaping—for the next forty-three years.

WALTER FREDERICK OSBORNE (1859–1903) A native of Dublin, Ireland, Walter Osborne was the son of animal painter William Osborne. He studied at the Royal Hibernian Academy in Dublin, then in Antwerp under Charles Verlat. His affectionate paintings of children and his loose brushstrokes have invited comparisons with Berthe Morisot's sensitive Impressionist work.

ALFRED WILLIAM PARSONS (1847–1920) A British landscape painter and illustrator, Parsons was born in Somerset, England. His love of painting flowers led him to garden design and horticulture, which he enjoyed at Luggers Hall, his Broadway estate. Frank Millet named his youngest son, John Alfred Parsons Millet, after his good friends John Singer Sargent and Alfred Parsons.

THEODORE ROBINSON (1852–1896) Born in Irasburg, Vermont, Robinson was one of the first American painters to travel to Giverny and one of the few to befriend Monet. Although Robinson was never his pupil, Monet offered to critique his paintings, and the two worked closely together from 1888 to 1892. Robinson's Giverny paintings are charming portraits of people outdoors, bathed in color and light, set among the beautiful walled gardens, stone footbridges, winding roads and rising hillsides of the village that so enchanted him.

AUGUSTUS SAINT-GAUDENS (1848–1907) The son of a French shoemaker and an Irish mother, Saint-Gaudens was born in Dublin, Ireland, and moved to New York with his family when he was six months old. Completing school at thirteen, he apprenticed to a cameo cutter and attended Cooper Union and the National Academy of Design. When he was nineteen, he moved to Europe, where he continued to study classical art and architecture in Paris and Rome and began work as a professional sculptor. In 1880, back in New York, Saint-Gaudens received a public commission that brought him success and fame: a monument to the Civil War naval hero, Admiral David Farragut, which still stands in New York's Madison Square Park.

JOHN SINGER SARGENT (1856–1925) Sargent was a brilliant and successful painter. Born in Florence to American parents, he grew up abroad and learned to draw and paint at an early age. Recognizing his son's talent, his father arranged for him to study portraiture under Carolus-Duran in Paris. Sargent was a friend of Monet, and the two artists exhibited together and collected each other's work. In 1886, Sargent decided to settle in London and moved into Whistler's old studio on Tite Street. He traveled extensively around the world, capturing in oil and watercolors the scenic places he visited and the friends and family who traveled with him.